Midnight in the Mountains

Midnight

in the Mountains

written by JULIE LAWSON

illustrations by SHEENA LOTT

ORCA BOOK PUBLISHERS

It's quiet in the mountains.
So quiet, I hear the hush of falling snow.

Mom and Dad are asleep.
Patrick is asleep.
Trouble is asleep. For once, he doesn't snore.

But I'm too excited to sleep.
Tonight is my first night in the mountains!

It's quiet in the mountains.
So quiet, I hear the brush of wings.

This morning we made snow angels.

We tried to build a snowman. We tried to have a snowball fight. But in the mountains, snow is powdery. It floated from our hands like the fluffy seeds of fireweed.

So we lay on our backs in deep, deep snow, sweeping arms and legs back and forth. Soon the frozen lake in front of our cabin was bright with angels.

"Mine are winged monsters," said Patrick.

I pointed to a shape that looked like a huge abominable snowman. "How did you make that?"

Patrick laughed. "That's Trouble."

It's quiet in the mountains.
So quiet, I hear the cold.

So cold, the snow squeaked when we walked on it.

So cold, my eyelashes tickled with frost.

Trouble dashed around, trying to keep his paws out of the snow. His fur got tangled with icicles. The cold made him sneeze.

Mom worried about frostbite.

How does frost bite? I wonder. How cold is the coldest cold? Cold enough to make frost flowers. I saw them today, draping the branches like lacy shawls. I saw ice crystals too, dancing in the sun.

It's quiet in the mountains.
Quiet as the color white.

Today we counted three colors. Blue, black and white.

"We forgot rainbows," I said.

Patrick gave me a funny look. "We haven't seen a rainbow."

I pointed to the row of icicles hanging from the eaves of our cabin. Rainbows shimmered in the sunlight.

Dad broke off an icicle and gently tapped the others, making music in the ice.

It's quiet in the mountains.
So quiet, I hear the rush of a fast-moving stream.

After lunch we walked along a frozen creek. In some places the wind had swept the snow away. The ice was so clear, we could see stones on the bottom. Fish darted in and out of the weeds and through the icy currents.

"Trouble's walking on water," I said.

Slip, slide, *wheeeeee …!*

And Trouble was gone, flat-out, across the creek.

It's quiet in the mountains. So quiet …
It wasn't this afternoon.

Yap yap yap! The huskies barked and pranced with excitement.

The musher harnessed them to the dogsled and tucked us in. Then he stood at the back and shouted, "Hie! Hie! Hie!" The dogs stopped barking and sped off across the lake.

"Gee, gee!" They turned to the right.

"Haw, haw!" And then to the left.

I looked over my shoulder and laughed. "Look at Trouble trying to catch up! He wants to be a sled dog, too!"

Poor Trouble. We left him behind in no time.

It's quiet in the mountains.
So quiet, I hear …
Is that a wolf howling? Way off in the distance?
I shiver. Should I wake the others?
No.
I hug the sound, the secret, to myself.

I wonder what secrets the huskies know about wolves and snow and mountains. I wonder if the wolves understand their language. Maybe the huskies were calling to the wolves, "Come set us free!" Maybe the wolf is coming, right now, to the rescue.

I hear a tiny sound from Trouble.
Maybe he's dreaming of wolves.

Tomorrow we're skiing around the lake. Patrick says it's easy. I can't wait to try.

But first, as soon as I get up, I'll check the snow for tracks.

After that I'll make snow angels and winged monsters and a whole xylophone of rainbow ice. Then I'll go exploring in the woods, with Trouble leading the way.

Who knows what we'll see?

Now I stare out the window and watch the snow.
I love it in the mountains.
It's so quiet.

So quiet, I think I hear the earth breathe.
I'm sure I hear the crackle of stars.
I know I hear the hush
of new-fallen
snow.

For my Aunt Lillian, who loved the mountains.

J.L.

To Nick, Nathan, Fraser and Chelsea,
who are always willing to strap on a backpack
and help me search for the ultimate painting.

S.L.

Text copyright © 1998 Julie Lawson
Illustration copyright © 1998 Sheena Lott

Canadian Cataloguing in Publication Data
Lawson, Julie, 1947 -
Midnight in the mountains

ISBN 1-55143-113-0

I. Lott, Sheena, 1950 -   II. Title.

PS8573.A94M52 1998 jC813' .54 C98 - 910399 - 4

PZ7. L4195Mi 1998

Library of Congress Catalog Card Number: 98 - 85282

Orca Book Publishers gratefully acknowledges the support of our publishing programs provided by the following agencies: the Department of Canadian Heritage, The Canada Council for the Arts, and the British Columbia Arts Council.

Design by Christine Toller

Printed and bound in Hong Kong

Orca Book Publishers
PO Box 5626, Station B
Victoria, BC Canada
V8R 6S4

Orca Book Publishers
PO Box 468
Custer, WA USA
98240-0468

98 99 00   5 4 3 2 1